# The Fear Of Night

The ghost in the night makes everyone fright.

Shashwat Shukla and Mohammad Ishan Khan

ISBN 978-93-5667-835-4
© Shashwat Shukla and Mohammad Ishan Khan 2023

Published in India 2023 by Pencil

**Contributors:**
Co-Author: Ramendra Shukla
Co-Author: Yash Pandey

*A brand of*
One Point Six Technologies Pvt. Ltd.
Unit no. 26, Ground Floor, Building A1,
Wadala Truck Terminal Road,
Near Post Office, Antop Hill, Mumbai - 400037
**E** connect@thepencilapp.com
**W** www.thepencilapp.com

# Author biography

## Biography of Shashwat

I am only 14 years old who created this story with help of his school friend Ishan, I didn't wote a book before this is my first book and I started to write book because one day I was watching television and I saw a girl who wrote a book and sold almost 1000 copies of it. Afterthat I also decided to write a book;We started in this 2022 and completed in 2023 we covered this book in a long time.

## Biography Of Ishan

I am also only 14 years old but just a month bigger than him, it is also my first book and by coincidence me and Shashwat watched the same show to get the idea to write a story. We had decided to upload this story on January 2023 but we got little late; You must be thinking that why it took 12 months to write this book the reason is examinations there are four examinations each after 3 months and there is so much of syllabus that's why we took so time.

# CONTENTS

# The Fear Of Night

**Narrator: There was a boy Kelvin his life was very normal he does a part-time job at a restaurant and he earn money for his mother, but once a weird incident happened when he was going his home at night from the restaurant.**

Kelvin: OK Boss I'm going it is 8 o'clock.

Boss: Yesterday you left early therefore you have to work for extra 3 hours.

Kelvin: But Boss!

Boss: Do your work or I will fire you!

Kelvin: Ok Boss.

**Narrator: Then he worked for 3 hours and left the restaurant. But when he was returning his home, he saw that due to some work the road was blocked with barriers.**

Kelvin: Oh no! Now what can I do……… let's take a shortcut, I am too hungry.

**(Then the Kelvin take the shortcut and then a weird thing happened, there was a boy coming to him and said," Run from here quickly!)**

Kelvin: What happened, tell me.

Boy: First run from here.

**(Then both of them sat at the scooter and parked near a house)**

Kelvin: Ok now tell me what happened.

Boy: My name is Peter. But first let's go to your house because I can't tell everything here.

**(HOME SCENE)**

Kelvin's Mother: Oh! It is 12 pm where is Kelvin, I should go to the police station.

**(Kelvin's scene)**

Kelvin: So, you can come with me.

**Narrator: Then both of them went in the Kelvin's home.**

Kelvin: Welcome to my house.

Peter: What a nice house.

Kelvin: Where is your house.

Peter: Actually, my house was destroyed.

Kelvin: How?

Peter: I was sleeping in my house and when I waked up I was near a river, and then I was going to my home and I saw that my home was disappear and I can't find my mother and father, and then I felt that someone is watching me then I heard a sound that was coming from the place of my house" Fear" then I ran from there and then I found a house similar to my house, but I saw that someone was watching me from the window of the house, and I ran in fear and I saw an old shop suddenly I saw a girl behind me saying " Fear of night " and then I met you.

Kelvin: Ah sorry! I do not know about it.

**(POLICE STATION SCENE)**

**Narrator: The mother reached the police station but it was closed then she decided to go back but there a sudden noise and she disappeared.**

**(HOME SCENE)**

**Narrator: Both of them switched on the lights.**

Kelvin: Where is mom. Oh god I have to call her.

**Narrator: Then he called her mom but when Kelvin called.**

Kelvin: Hello! Mom.

**Narrator: Then a weird sound came from the phone like someone is screaming "Aaaaaaaaaa.." then it said Network problem.**

Peter: What happened!

Kelvin: My mother is not here and she is not answering my phone.

**(The bell rings)**

Kelvin: Oh mom! Thank God you are back let us now have dinner.

Mom: Oh, who are you.

Peter:  I am Peter Kelvin's friend.

Mom: Oh, Kelvin, you didn't tell me about him.

Kelvin: Mom he is my new friend.

Mom: Oh, ok let's eat dinner.

Kelvin: Oh, mom you forgot I told you to buy vegetables did you buy.

Mom: Oh, sorry I forgot but no problem I will make it.

**Narrator: Then the mother makes the food with something that looks weird.**

Kelvin: Mom what is this dish.

Peter: I think that it is Spanish dish.

**Narrator: Then the mother said in deep dark loud voice.**

Mom: It is my dish.

**Narrator: Then both of them went to sleep and when they wake up, they saw they are in another house, they make a round of house then the Peter spoke.**

Peter: It is my house.

Kelvin: What! How can be it possible you said that your house was destroyed.

**Narrator: Both of them came I fear and rush to find the exit but suddenly they realized that there is no exit, suddenly a sound came Grrrrrrr… and Kelvin fell down into a secret tunnel.**

Kelvin: Help! Help! Peter, please help me!

Peter: Where from this sound came, I should check.

**Narrator: Suddenly Peter saw again Girl with red hand. Peter ran and ran and he saw the girl every around him that was girl, he found the Kelvin and girl said in very loud scary sound, "You have to answer my riddle to get out the house".**

Peter and Kelvin: Ok.

Girl: I am scary when you have more of me, you will see only less. What's it.

Peter: I didn't know.

**(Kelvin and Peter thought for some time suddenly the girl spoke;)**

Girl: You have 2 minutes otherwise I will kill you!

Peter: I do not want to die; Kelvin, please try to answer the riddle.

Kelvin: Oh, I know that.

Peter: Tell fast only 10 seconds left!!!!

Kelvin: It is Aaaaaaaaaa……

Peter: What happened!

Kelvin: I have a heart disease; I cannot tell that word.

Peter: Please Kelvin try to speak please!!!!!

**(Only 3 seconds left, at the last second Kelvin spoke in loud voice,)**

Kelvin: Darkness!!!!

**(When Kelvin said this word, they were outside the house and Kelvin was fine then they rush to their home.)**

**(When they reach the home, they found the Kelvin's mother was not there.)**

Kelvin: Where is my mother.

Peter: I don't know.

Kelvin: Let's find outside the house.

Peter: Ok.

**(They went off the house to find the Kelvin's mother.)**

Kelvin: She is not outside the house, let us find my mother from my scooter.

Peter: Ok.

**(They look for the mother for 1 hour but could not find her)**

Kelvin: Oh no! Now I have to go police station.

Peter: But why.

Kelvin: To report that my mom is missing.

Peter: I am very tired.

**(Then they reached police station and they call police, but there was no one suddenly a sound came "Fear" and a police man came from below of the table.)**

Police: What do you want.

Kelvin: My mom is missing.

Police: Did you are able to see.

Kelvin: Yes, Why?

Police: It is 11 am and it is clear written on the notice that police station close till 11 am.

Kelvin: Please! Help me!

Police: No means no.

Kelvin: If you will not help, I will talk to your senior about your behavior.

**(When Kelvin said this a loud sound came and his scooter blast!)**

Kelvin: What the hell is this!

**(Then the police man said get out otherwise I will kill you! Then the lights switched off.)**

Peter: What is this happening. Kelvin please let's go.

Kelvin: Ok Fast! Fast!

**Narrator: Then both of them went to home.**

Kelvin: What can we do now.

Peter: Calm down we will find your mother.

**(The bell rings)**

Kelvin: Who is there.

**(A loud sound came Aaaa……)**

Peter: What is this sound. I am very scared.

**Narrator: Then both of them opened the door.**

Police: Hi!

Kelvin: Why do you came to house?

Peter: And how you found the address of here?

Police: I was following you, and when I heard the conversation between you, I felt that I have done wrong so I am here to found your mother.

Kelvin: Thank you brother.

**Narrator: Then the Kelvin told him all the matter and police man said ok you have to come with me.**

Kelvin: Ok no problem.

Police: How does your mother look like?

Kelvin: See this picture.

**Narrator: When the police saw the picture he shocked and spoke.**

Police: I have seen this woman in my friend's police station, she came to complain but the police station was locked.

Kelvin: Which complain?

Police: She came to report that his son is missing.

Kelvin: What was the name of son?

 Police: I think she said that her son's name is Kelvin.

Kelvin: Wait! I am kelvin!

Police: Oh! I had seen that in morning 7 am she had gone somewhere in the forest.

Peter: Ok Kelvin let's go!

Kelvin: My mom said that something is scary there.

Police: What scary?

Peter: Yes what?

Kelvin: She said that anyone has gone there never come back.

Police: What! If it is then we have to find your mother quickly.

**Narrator: Then all of them went to the forest and they saw a girl she said that play with me.**

Kelvin: Who are you?

Girl: I said to play with me otherwise I will kill you.

Peter: Ok I will play with but what is your name.

**Narrator: Suddenly the thunderstorm occurred and girl move his head up and when they saw him Peter spoke that it was that girl, then all of them ran to save their lives but then Kelvin said-**

Kelvin : We are here to find my mother not to run.

Peter: Yes!

Police: There is someone sitting there.

Kelvin: Let check it out.

Police: Please show us your face.

**Narrator: When she showed her face, they were shocked because it was Kelvin's mother.**

Kelvin: Mom is that you?

**Narrator: Then the mother said in dark voice.**

Mom: Yes, it is me my son.

Peter: Kelvin don't go close to her I am afraid.

Mom: Why are you afraid my son's friend?

**Narrator: Then Peter tries to spoke but his voice was not coming out.**

Police: What are you saying?

**Narrator: Then the lightning fell on Kelvin's mother and she vanished.**

**(Kelvin cries)**

Kelvin: Mom! Mom! Nooooooooooooooooo!

Peter: Kelvin don't cry your mom will back.

Kelvin: How but how do you not see that lightning fell on my mother?

Peter: Yes, I saw that.

Police: Can I tell a thing.

Kelvin: Now what is left to say?

Police: Lightning fell on your mother and she disappeared but if a lighting fell on any people, he\she doesn't disappear. He\she lay down there and faint.

Peter: Then why the Kelvin's mom disappeared?

**Narrator: Then a sound came and all of them came in fear because it is like that someone is calling them!**

Police: Who is there?

**Narrator: Then a sound came and it said" Your mother's killer".**

Kelvin: What?

Peter: From where this sound is coming?

Police: It is very big forest so we can't find because in this everyone's voice will be eco if he/she speaks loudly.

Peter: No problem! Let us find in different direction.

Police: What are you mad this forest area is 100 km!

Peter: Oh! I am sorry.

Police: We shall go home now!

Kelvin: Nice idea brother, but if both of you want to go then you can I will find my mother and then I will come back.

Police: Have you lost your mind!

Kelvin: Yes, I have lost everything my mom my mind all.

**Narrator: By saying this Kelvin ran off in the forest and Peter and Police were running to find him.**

**Both police and Peter were in hurry because anything can happen in that forest.**

Peter: Hey! Did you find kelvin?

Police: No! And you?

Peter: No!

Police: We have travelled only small distance this forest is very big.

Peter: Idea!

Police: What?

Peter: Let's call him the ring will rang so we can find him he can't go so far.

Police: Yes, nice idea do you know his number?

Peter: I didn't know last one digit.

Police: No problem, we will call on every number.

**Narrator: Then both of them called on every last number from 0 to 9 all the numbers from 0 to 8 were wrong now they know that his number ends with 9.**

**Police: Can you hear the sound?**

Peter: No.

Police: It means he had gone very in the forest.

Peter: Then how can we find him?

Police: Last time we had seen him he had gone in South direction.

Peter: So, what?

Police: Did he have a disease like problem in breathing, walking?

Peter: He have a heart disease.

Police: Then we have lost him backwards.

Peter: How?

Police: In this forest there are various type of animals that attacks a single person. Now we are being watched by animals but we are together so they are not attacking. And Kelvin had heart disease so the animal came front in Kelvin and he faint.

Peter: Yes, it can be but it is getting to night so it is better to go home, can you please stay in home I am very afraid.

Police: Ok no problem.

**Narrator: Then both of them went home but when they reached home, they were shocked someone was sitting on the chair.**

Police: Who is there?

**Narrator: Then a sound came and it rotate his neck at 180' angle and Peter spoke she is my mother.**

Police: What!

Peter: Yes, she is my mother.

Police: But how can be this possible?

Peter: What how do you know?

Police: When I came to your house and you gone to drank water then I asked Kelvin about you.

Peter: Oh.

**Narrator: Then the mother said-**

Mother: Hey why you have come to my house if anyone enter my house, I eat him.

Police: You are in the forest not in the house.

**Narrator: Then suddenly someone hit the mother's head.**

Peter: Who is there?

**Narrator: Then suddenly they realize that someone is behind them and when they saw him, he was Kelvin.**

**Peter: Kelvin where were you?**

Kelvin: When I ran from there, I thought that if there were many animals in the forest so how I will survive, and then I thought about you that are you fine or not so I ran to find you and when I was finding you, I saw a wolf so I took up the rod to scare him, and I heard the loud voice and came here.

Police: But why you ran?

Kelvin: I was angry and I can't stop myself from doing that all, sorry for that.

**Narrator: Suddenly someone knock the door.**

Kelvin: Who is there?

**Narrator: Then they opened the door and saw that there was no one, they were thinking that someone is doing joke with them.**

Police: Can you please give me glass of water.

Peter: Sure.

**Narrator: Then it was night the Peter said to police to stay with them.**

Kelvin: Why Peter now I am here.

Peter: You have a heart disease If anyone come suddenly in front of you it is chance that you can got heart attack so if he will here so we can take you to the hospital.

Kelvin: Ok.

Police: Ok so let's sleep it is 9'o clock.

**Narrator: Then all of them slept and when they woke up, they were going to what is in the Forest.**

Police: Wear this it will protect you from animals.

Peter & Kelvin: Ok.

Peter: Can I take the food.

Kelvin: Sure.

Kelvin: Why are you taking these rockets.

Police: These are special rockets we have to take one if any of us lost anywhere then he will pull this label and rocket will go up and other will find him.

Kelvin: Oh!

Peter: I have taken the food.

Kelvin: Ok I am taking the water.

**Narrator: Then after doing things they went on to the Forest.**

Police: So now be alert.

Peter:  Ok!

Police: Shhh! Speak slowly.

Peter: Oh sorry.

Kelvin: Let's go.

**Narrator: Then they went into the forest after 2 days they find Kelvin's mother in the middle of the forest hanging on the tree.**

Police: There she is.

Kelvin: Yes, but how?

Peter: What?

Kelvin: My mom said that she can't climb tree.

Police: Looks that an animal has chased your mother and to get rid of him she climbs up the tree.

Kelvin: Ok let's take my mother to hospital.

Police: Ok but from where we came.

Kelvin: We came from south but where is South I didn't know. Peter, give me the compass.

Peter: I forgot to bring compass.

Kelvin: What!

**Narrator: Sudden it starts thundering and the lightning fell on one tree and whole forest came to burn.**

Police: How it started thundering?

Police: We have to get out of here.

Peter: But how we are surrounded with fire.

Police: Don't worry for this situation I have fire extinguisher.

Kelvin: What when you had taken it.

Police: You forgot that I am a police man.

Kelvin: Oh!

**Narrator: Then they went to the hospital with Kelvin's mother.**

Doctor: I can't believe this!

Kelvin: What?

Doctor: Your mother has black blood!

Peter: I think because lightning struck on your mother.

Doctor: No that's not possible if it will be then your mother should have less blood.

Police: I know why this is going on that forest is dangerous. Because when I enter the forest, I saw your mother flying in air I was not telling you because you both will come in fear and she was also saying some like "Fear of Night".

**Narrator: Then Peter and Kelvin were shocked.**

Peter: Is that what I am thinking.

Kelvin: Yes.

**Narrator: Then kelvin take a rod and hit policeman's head and policeman fainted.**

Doctor: What have you done this?

Peter: You don't believe that we met ghost 3 times and every time it says fear of night and he also said it because he is also possessed.

Doctor: What!

Peter: Yes, you can also see that his eyes is full black!

Kelvin: Now come with me let's go in it's deep.

**Narrator: Then policeman shouted very loudly and died.**

Kelvin: All run outside of hospital because his soul is coming out.

(Next Day)

Peter: Now what can we do Kelvin? We had lost our partner.

Kelvin: I said that I will go in deep and think about it.

Doctor: What do you mean?

Kelvin: We have gone to the forest and returned safely I thought then how can it be because if anyone goes to the forest, he/she die But I and Peter didn't, it mean there is something from which we came back.

Peter: Yes! I had a piece of stone.

Kelvin: What! did you have it now?

Peter: No, I left my bag at the hospital.

Kelvin: If we have to know what that stone is then we have to go that hospital and doctor you have to also come.

Doctor: Why?

Kelvin: Because you know more than us about the hospital.

Doctor: Ok! I am ready.

(In the hospital)

Kelvin: Doctor where is that room?

Doctor: Room no. 225 at 5th floor.

Peter: What we have to go to the top.

Doctor: Yes! We have to go with lift.

Kelvin: No  no, if we go from lift then we can stuck.

Peter: I saw someone.

Kelvin: Who?

Peter: I think he is that policeman.

**Narrator: Then suddenly a stone fell from the window and that was what they were finding.**

Kelvin: Ok! We have got the stone let's go.

Police: I gave you one thing now I will take one thing.

**Narrator: Then policeman came he caught doctor and he and doctor vanished and Peter and Kelvin rush to their home.**

Kelvin: Now we are safe.

Peter: Now we can find what is the root of this big problem.

Kelvin: But now it is getting dark so we have to sleep and we have to tie this stone to us so it will protect us.

### (MORNING)

**Narrator: When Kelvin wakes up, he saw that Peter is not there and he gone everywhere to find Peter.**

Kelvin: Oh! Where is Peter?

**Narrator: Then a sound came like someone was screaming.**

**Aaaaaaaaaa....**

Kelvin: Who is that?

**Narrator: Then Kelvin smells very bad smell. Then suddenly light goes off and Kelvin sees that there was blood everywhere.Then suddenly a girl came in front of him.**

Girl: Give me that stone and I will give you your friend back.

**Narrator: Kelvin was frightened so he can't make any decision and he gave stone to the girl and then she disappeared and he saw Peter sleeping on bed.**

Kelvin: Peter wake up wake up.

Peter: What happened?

Kelvin: Did you imagine anything.

Peter: No but why?

Kelvin: We don't have stone right now. Someone said that he had captured you.

Peter: What?

Kelvin: I think we have to go to that hospital for more information.

Peter: But it is dangerous!

Kelvin: Yes, it is but I am tired from it, so I want its end.

Peter: Ok, let's go.

**Narrator: They both went to hospital and gone to that room 225.**

Kelvin: Peter see there is hidden lever.

Narrator: When Kelvin pushed the liver a secret room opened.

Peter: Whoa! What happened.

Kelvin: I think this is a secret room.

**Narrator: When Kelvin and Peter entered the room they found that there is a television covered with a cloth and was kept at the corner of the room.**

Peter: See that telvision.

Kelvin: Yes, let's check out.

Peter: What is this cuboid?

Kelvin: Peter, It is a video tape!

Peter: What I had never saw it.

Kelvin: Yes, because it is now not in use.

Peter: I an eager to know that what is inside it.

Kelvin: Peter don't be so excited because there is policeman in this building.

Peter: Oh no.

Kelvin: First let's check out this video.

**Narrator: When they saw the video they became frightened because when the video ended policeman came behind them.**

Policeman: Caught you.

Kelvin: Peter listen I have a plan when I say three you should climb up on my back.

Peter: But why so?

Kelvin: Do you want to live or die.

Peter: Fine.

**Narrator: When the kelvin said three Peter climbed up on his back and Kelvin took out the stone from his pocket.**

Peter: What! You had said that you had given the stone to the girl.

Kelvin: I had given her the fake stone.

Peter: Oh.

Kelvin: Now we can search all around the hospital.

Policeman: You have the sone that's why I can't catch you otherwise I would tear you both down into pieces.

Kelvin: Let's go Peter.

**Narrator: Then they searched all around hospital and foud that there is an dead body in each room and when they saw the last room they found found a time bomb which was going to explode in 1 minute.**

Kelvin: Peter come on run.

**Narrator: They ran with their all efforts and were able to get out of the hospital and when the time completed there was a large sound saying Fear of**

**night and the hospital exploded.**

Peter: Kelvin now what we will do.

Kelvin: You had saw that television.

Peter: Yes.

Kelvin: Behind that television there was another video tape, see here it is.

Peter: Oh.

Kelvin: Let's go to home to watch this video tape.

**Narrator: Then both of them went to home.**

Peter: Let's watch this clip.

**Narrator: When they were watching video clip Kelvin shouted.**

Kelvin: No, noo.

Peter: What happened?

Kelvin: You didn't saw?

Peter: What?

Kelvin: See there is a man going and when he reached the pole he disappeared.

Peter: Let's rewind the clip and watch.

Kelvin: See there.

Peter: Yes, but how is this possible.

**Narrator: When the video ended Kelvin took out the video tape he saw that there are some numbers written on it.**

Kelvin: Peter come here.

Peter: Yes, what happened?

Kelvin: See there are some numbers written on it.

Peter: Yes, let me check; The numbers are 2010.

Kelvin: What can be 2010?

Peter: I think it could be a car number plate.

Kelvin: It colud be but it is not so appropriate that a car can have number plate of just 10 years before.

Peter: Oh It can be a year.

Kelvin: Yes, it means this man will be still alive.

Peter: But how can we find him?

Kelvin: Let's check the video tape again maybe we can get the address.

**Narrator: When they were going to see the video tape again it blasted.**

Peter: What happened?

Kelvin: How did it blasted?

Peter: See there is something written on television.

**Narrator: The text that was written on television was,"You had cheated me now I won't leave you".**

Kelvin: What how can we cheat the television?

**Narrator: Suddenly that girl appeared in front of them.**

Girl: Not we only you had cheated me.

Kelvin: What!

Girl: You had given me the fake stone and cheated me now I can't do anything to you but I can do a thing.

Peter: What?

**Narrator: Then the girl shoted loudly and Kelvin's house and the girl disappeared.**

Kelvin: What was that!

Peter: Kelvin let's run because i think we are not safe here we have to go to another city.

**Narrator: They left for the city in the early morning so that they reach a city before evening.**

Peter: Kelvin, its getting dark how far we have to go.

Kelvin: According to this map about only 500 metres.

**Narrator: They found a city which was full of light they were very tired so they knocked the door of a house from which and old man came out.**

Old man: Yes how can I help you?

Kelvin: We had came from another city and we are very tired and hungry so can we stay in your house for a night.

Old man: Yes, of course.

**Narrator: Then the onld man provided a meal and a bed to them for sleep.**

Peter: Sir, if you don't mind can I ask a question from you?

Old man: Yes.

Peter: Why do you allow us to enter your house without knowing our names?

Old man: Good question, I am living in this house since 30 years and since 30 years my children didn't came even to see my face they only send me money for my daily use.

Kelvin: Its very bad.

Old man: After 30 years when you came to my house I thought my own children had came that's why I had allow you to enter my house, by the way what is your name.

Peter: My name is Peter.

Kelvin: And my name is Kelvin.

Old man: What a coincidence.

Kelvin: What coincidence.

Peter: Let me guess your children name are also Kelvin and Peter.

Old man: Yes you guessed right. It means that you are my own children then I will treat you as my sons.

Kelvin: Thank you because my father died before I born.

Old man: Oh sorry!

Kelvin: No problem, because he was a better and he set a bet that took his live and he had also gone to jail and also he beat my mother very much that's why I hate him.

Old man: Ok now it's 10o'clock let's sleep.

Kelvin: Good Night.

Peter: Sweet dreams.

Old man: What a nice chldren, Good night.

Peter: Kelvin wake up.

Kelvin: What its only 4o'clock.

Peter: I saw there something.

Kelvin: Let's check.

**Narrator: There was old man siiting on the bed a drawing room and was doing exercise.**

Kelvin: Sir, what are you doing.

Old man: Good morning. I am doing exercise.

Kelvin: At night.

Old man: I know that you don't have habit to wake up early therefore I didn't wake you up.

Peter: Oh Kelvin let's go to sleep.

Kelvin: No Peter we should also exercise.

Peter: Good idea.

Old man: Thank you beacuse my children had never exercised with me.

Kelvin: That's fine.

**Narrator: After exercising they came back to room and they shared their problem to the old man.**

Old man: What! Is this happened to you?

Kelvin: Yes!

Old man: I had also suffered from it.

Kelvin: How?

Old man: My mother also died because my father was a killer and he killed a man who became a ghost and killed my mother and father.

Kelvin: Then afterthat you may come out of that issue.

Old man: No, the ghost did't stoped it killed my all relatives but I was out of country that's why I remained safe.

Kelvin: Then how can we get out of this problem.

Old man: It is only starting the real picture hasn't started yet.

Peter: What do you mean?

Old man: If you have to get out of the trouble then you have to go at a place.

Kelvin: Which place?

Old man: You have travel to the middle of the Atlantic ocean.

Peter: What! But there is only water.

Old man: All know that there is water in middle of Atlantic ocean but when you will go to that place you have to say a magic word,"Oi-ka-fee".

Kelvin: What is Oi-ka-fee?

Old man: It is a small area which drowned inside the ocean and never explored by any scientist.

Peter: No, Atlantis is discovered by scientist.

Old man: When I talked about Atlantis? There is a small area just beside it about 40 km far.

Kelvin: Ok, but what will happen when we will say "Oi-ka-fee".

Old man: You will find it when you will reach there.

**Narrator: Then they both setted up there bags.**

Kelvin: Sir, will you come with us.

Old man: Sure I will but give me a minute.

Peter: Kelvin, have you ever heard about that area before.

Kelvin: No, I had heard it first time.

Old man: Ok let's go.

Peter: Where had you gone.

Old man: I had gone to take my medicines and food.

Peter: Oh.

Kelvin: Peter, have you kept all things.

Peter: Yes, and see these are the rockets which will tell us where we are.

Kelvin: Are these are the rockets given by the policeman.

Peter: Yes.

Old man: But there are only two rockets.

Kelvin: Sir, you can take one rocket me and Peter will be together.

Old man: Thank you.

**Narrator: Then they went to the coast.**

Peter: Which boat we should take.

Kelvin: I think we should take a covered boat because if unfortunately rain happened then we will be wet.

Peter: See there.

Old man: What?

Peter: There is a yellow coloured boat.

Kelvin: Yes!

**Narrator: Then all of them sat at the boat and set a sail to the middle of the Atlantic ocean.**

Peter: I think we have must travelled 1000 miles because of this problem.

Kelvin: Yes, we travelled to hospital, police station, forest, another city and now to the middle of the ocean.

Old man: I wonder you travelled so much but there is not even a sprain or cut in your body.

Kelvin: Yes because we got a stone which was protecting us.

Old man: Can you show me the stone.

Kelvin: Of course. See this.

Old man: Let me check my information is correct or not.

Peter: What do you mean.

Old man: I mean whether this stone is inster or not.

Kelvin: What is inster.

Old man: It is a name given to the rocks which gives positive energy.

Peter: But how positive energy can help us.

Old man: The souls or we can say ghost are only made up of negative energy and when they come in contract with positive energy the get vanished.

Kelvin: Oh, that's why none of the ghosts attacked us.

**Narrator: Then the old man put some chemical on stone and it changed into the dark blue colour.**

Peter: Wow! It is a colour changing stone.

Old man: This dark blue colour shows it contain positive energy and if it had converted into dark green then it contains negative energy.

**Narrator: Next day inthe afternoon they reached the middle of the ocean.**

Peter: Wow! This look amazing.

Kelvin: We have to say something to open this door, but I don't remember it.

Old man: I know that it will happen that's why I kept I diary in which I have written that word.

Kelvin: Oh Thank you.

**Narrator: Then the old man gave diary to Kelvin and he shouted loudly.**

Kelvin: Oi-ka-fee.

**Narrator: By saying this a plant inside the ocean dragged them into a cave.**

Peter: What! There is no water here.

Old man: Yes I taught you that know.

Kelvin: Let's move forward.

Narrator: Then all of them went forward in the cave.

Kelvin: Hmmmmm. It semms that no one had came here before.

Peter: Yes, because it is beneath the ocean.

**Narrator: At that moment the old man jumped over them.**

Kelvin: What are you doing?

**Narrator: After that  a dripstone fell just behind them.**

Peter: Thank you.

Old man: We should be careful in this cave because it is full of dangers like falling dripstone, lava land, lazers and monsters.

Kelvin: Ok we will be careful now, but how we will know that where we have to go.

Old man: Kelvin give me that stone.

Kelvin: Ok, but what will you do?

Old man: Just watch me.

**Narrator: Then he put the stone on the ground and after a minute the stone pointed upwards.**

Peter: Why is it pointing upwards?

**Narrator: And when they saw up they were shocked because there were animal footprints at the top.**

Peter: What! how can there be footprints?

Old man: I think it is the place of mythical creature called Tretoix.

Kelvin: Tretoix, I have never heard about it.

Old man: Tretoix is a creature that has 8 legs, two of lion, two of tiger, two of horse and two of wolf.

Peter: What!

Old man: Yes and this creature always walk on the ceiling.

Peter: Is that creature still alive?

Old man: I am not sure about it but if I can reach there then I can tell how many years old the footprint is.

Kelvin: But how can we reach there, it is almost about three metres.

Old man: If we can bring that rock which is mostly about two metres then we can reach there but the problem is that it can be of thirty to thirty-five pounds.

Kelvin: We can do that.

Peter: How?

Kelvin: See the cave is so cold because its temperature is around 5 C and if the morning time temperature is 5 C then in night it will surely fall below 0 C which is freezing point of water.

Peter: But what can we do with the temperature.

Kelvin: We can't lift up rock but we can push it. If we reduce the friction then we can push it.

Old man: And how we will reduce the friction.

Kelvin: If we pour water on the floor then in night it will freeze and we will able to push it.

Peter: So for that we have wait till night.

### (NIGHT)

Kelvin: Peter, Peter, Wake up. There is no time to sleep, see the water had frozen.

Peter: Kelvin where is Sir?

Kelvin: What! I think he is with you.

Peter: No he wasn't with me.

Kelvin: Then we have to search him.

**Narrator: Then they both went to find the old man and after searching for 5 to 10 minutes Peter saw a shadow.**

Peter: Kelvin see that shadow.

Kelvin: I think he is sir.

**Narrator: When they went to that shadow they were shocked there was Tretoix eating an animal and the old man was trapped in a cage.**

Kelvin: Peter we have to free sir.

Peter: But how this creature is looking so dangerous.

Kelvin: Peter everyone have one fear that everyone is afrid of so if we came to know about his fear then we can free sir.

Peter: I think this creature can only hear sound because he had caputred sir but not us.

Kelvin: Then what from that.

Peter: I think when we were sleeping the sir had made an sound and had been captured so if I create a sound then he will follow me and in that time you can free sir.

Kelvin: But are you sure you can beat him otherwise I can do the same job.

Peter: I can beat him.

**Narrator: Then at going one corner Peter shouted loudly and in few second Tretiox started to chase him and within that time Kelvin arrived before old man.**

Old man: Kelvin, thank you for coming.

Klevin: Sir this is not good time to talk, we should first escape from here.

**Narrator: Then after a few tries Kelvin broke the lock.**

Old man: Where is Peter.

Kelvin: He will be here soon.

Peter: It was very difficult.

Old man: What happened?

Kelvin: We will explain you later, first let's escape this cave.

**Narrator: Then they escaped the cave and came back on the boat.**

Peter: Now what we will do we got nothing information from that cave.

Old man: Why are you thinking that we got no information from the cave? We came to know about Tretoix and when I was trapped there is saw that there were a lot of shining gems there.

Kelvin: What!

Peter: I think he is there to protect the treasure.

Old man: Our food will over soon so we have to find a place because we can't go back.

**Narrator: Then after a day they saw an island.**

Peter: Yes we got an island.

Kelvin: We should be alert because here can be also some mythical creature.

Old man: See someone is there.

**Narrator: When Peter saw it closely he shouted.**

Peter: No no! Kelvin we have to move back.

Kelvin: Why?

Peter: See that red hand girl.

Kelvin: Rotate quickly, quickly rotate the boat.

**Narrator: It was about 6-7 metres when they returned back.**


**Narrator: Then all of them went back.**

Peter: Kelvin, I am hungry.

Old man: Our food is over.

Kelvin: What! Then what we will do now.

Old man: There is only one way we have to go on that island.

Peter: No way! It will kill us.

Old man: How it can kill you if you have the stone.

Peter: But you saw that it doesn't worked previous time.

Old man: It is because it was a creature not a ghost.

**Narrator: Just then thunderstorm occurred and all of them hurried to reach the island.**

Kelvin: Let us make a shed to protect us.

Peter: Kelvin who is that?

Kelvin: Oh no we have to get into shelter quickly, Sir come fast.

Old man: Yes, what happened?

Kelvin: First let's get into shelter.

**Narrator: It was very difficult for them to fight against the ghost and also one of them have to go outside in search of food.**

Kelvin: Ok I am going.

Old man: No you won't.

Kelvin: Let me go otherwise we will starve and die.

Old man: I will go because I had studied about that ghost, it need a meal to get calm, once it will eat me you should take things you need as it will calm down for two to three hours.

Peter: What you will sacrifice yourself! No way. You are important key.

Kelvin: Wait, first I want to know that how did you know all of that.


**Narrator: The old man laughed.**

Old man: Hmm..

**Narrator: Just then he makes his way out and shouted.**

Old man: Fear of Night.

**Narrator: Just then he got splattered into pieces.**

Peter: Kelvin I think we should get out of here quickly.

**Narrator: Then Peter heard that someone is calling him. Peter!**

Peter: Who's there?

Old man: It's me.

Peter: Oh my god!

Old man: You can't run away from me.

Peter: Kelvin stop.

**Narrator: But it was too late Kelvin stepped on a lever and they fell into a hole.**

Kelvin: What the hell!

Peter: Oh no! See there.

Kelvin: What?

Peter: He is Tretoix.

Kelvin: What are we in that cave again?

Peter: I think so.

**Narrator: Just then old man appeared in front of them.**

Old man: Hello.

Kelvin: What who are you?

Old man: You don't have to get afraid of me, I only want you to help me.

Peter: How can we help a ghost?

Old man: I have to take revenge.

Kelvin: From whom?

Old man: The one who killed my son and daughter-in-law, I got the information that someone has killed my son and daughter-in-law.

Kelvin: Did you know who is he?

Old man: I only know that the killer was a policeman. And he lived near a island.

Peter: So what can we help in that?

Old man: See I was looking for a person who is fearless, caring and have solution for everything and I saw all of these qualitites in you so I can get into your body and kill the killer.

Peter: But why you didn't took anyone else body.

Old man: Because you are my grandson Peter.

Peter: No way, you are lying.

Old man: You haven't met me anytime but I have met you once and from that I came everytime to see you.

Peter: If this is true then you can use my body because killer killed my mom and dad.

Kelvin: I will also come with you.

**Narrator: Then all of them travelled to that place.**

Old man: Now this is the time.

**Narrartor: Old man without wasting anytime get into the Peter's body.**

Old man: Let's go! But be careful.

**Narrator: They got into the house but the killer saw them and he pulled the lever from which Kelvin fell down.**

Old man: Kelvin! I have to take my revenge quickly otherwise the moon will set down and I will die.

Killer: Caught you. Now how you will escape.

**Narrator: The killer putted a net over it and he threw a powder from which his power decreased meanwhile Kelvin woke up.**

Kelvin: Where am I? What's that sound, i think the old man has been captured now I should help him.

**Narrator: He tried to climb the wall but his nail just broke.**

Kelvin: What the hell!

**Narrator: He was not able to climb the wall and just then he felt himself lighter and he came out of pit.**

Kelvin: It should only be sir who helped me now I should help him.

**Narrator: Kelvin serched for every room but he didn't found him but coincidensely he pushed a lever and secret room opened.**

Kelvin: Stay away otherwise I will kill you.

**Narrator: Then there was a intense fight and Kelvin at last he took a knife to kill him.**

Kelvin: No I will not kill you.

Killer: Thanks.

**Narrator: By saying this he cutted the net of old man and he woke up.**

Old man: I have been waiting this time since long time now I will take revenge of my son and daughter-in-law.

**Narrator: By saying this he took the knife and killed him.**

Old man: Now I am going.

Peter: Thank you because of you I also killed the killer of my mom and dad.

Old man: It was nice to be with you but now its time for leave. And Kelvin all of that was happening to both of you was done by me to take you both here.

Kelvin: So where is my mom.

Old man: Once you will go home you will find her.

**Narrator: By saying this old man flew up and disappeared and then Peter and Kelvin went back home.**